PATRICIA ST JOHN

The Other Kitten

Copyright © Patricia St John 1983
This edition revised 2007, reprinted 2009

ISBN 978 1 84427 290 7

Scripture Union
207–209 Queensway, Bletchley, Milton Keynes, MK2 2EB, England
Email: info@scriptureunion.org.uk
Website: www.scriptureunion.org.uk

Scripture Union Australia
Locked Bag 2, Central Coast Business Centre, NSW 2252
Website: www.scriptureunion.org.au

Scripture Union USA
PO Box 987, Valley Forge, PA 19482
Website: www.scriptureunion.org

British Library Cataloguing-in-Publication Data.
A catalogue record of this book is available from the British Library.

Printed and bound in Great Britain by Digital Book Print.

Cover design by Go Ballistic
Internal design and layout by Author and Publisher Services

Chapter one

Mark woke first and lay, still half asleep, trying to remember. Then he woke properly and it all came back to him. He jumped out of bed and ran to the window. He flung it wide open and stuck his head far out.

What a morning! The sun was just rising behind the trees at the bottom of the garden. The dew on the grass sparkled like silver, except for the golden patches where the daffodils grew. The birds were singing wildly, madly. Mark dressed quickly and opened his suitcase to see that nothing had been forgotten. He pushed aside the clothes that Mum had packed. First he checked the really important things: his swimming trunks, underwater goggles

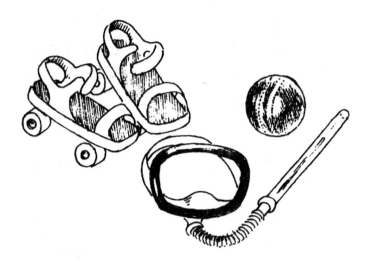

and snorkel (he was determined to swim, however much Gran said it was too cold). Then he checked his roller skates and cricket ball. His bat and shrimping net would be strapped to his case and he would carry his football under his arm. Everything was in order.

He thought he had better wake Carol in case she made them late, fussing over her packing. He went to her room where she lay asleep, her hair spread all over the pillow. He pulled the bedclothes off her and tweaked her toes. She sat up, started to be cross and then remembered too.

"It's today, isn't it?" she said.

"Of course, stupid! You don't think it's yesterday, do you?"

She ran to the window. "It's a lovely day," she said. "I'm going to say goodbye to the rabbits."

Carol had already packed her things the day before, leaving her spade and bucket on top of her case. She pulled on her jeans and shirt. Then she ran downstairs and into the garden. She picked some dandelion leaves as a goodbye present and disappeared round the corner of the house. Mark was left alone.

I'd better wake Mum and Dad, he thought. We've got to get to Gran's by

lunchtime and Mum and Dad take *so* long
to get dressed! He decided to take them
tea in bed. He made it very carefully,
warming the pot and pouring the milk into
the jug. When he reached his parents'
bedroom, he kicked the door open. His
mum and dad both opened their eyes,
blinked and yawned.

"What on earth do you think you're doing, Mark?" said Dad. "It's only quarter past six!"

Mark put the cups down on the bedside table.

"You said you wanted to start early," he said.

"I didn't mean *this* early!" said Dad with another yawn. But he and Mum sat up and drank their tea. It was cosy and still half dark in the bedroom. Mark suddenly wondered if he wanted to go away after all.

"You'll tell us when the baby comes, won't you?" he said. "I hope it's a boy. Carol's rubbish at cricket."

Mum laughed. "It can't be long now," she said. "But Carol wants a girl, so someone is going to be disappointed. Dad and I have decided to be pleased with

whatever comes. Anyhow, where is Carol?"

"Saying goodbye to the rabbits. Dad, you'd better get up, and you too, Mum. You take *ages* dressing. I'll make some toast."

Dad grumbled a little but decided that it would not hurt to start early. "The sooner we go, the sooner I'll come back," he said to Mum as he began shaving.

Mark had made the toast long before his parents had finished upstairs. They appeared at last and Carol came in from the garden, sniffing and looking sad.

"I'll take great care of your rabbits, Carol," said Mum, "so don't worry. There'll be wild rabbits in the field opposite Gran's."

"And squirrels in the wood," said Dad.

"And lambs at the farm," said Carol, cheering up.

"And the old horse who sticks his head over the gate," said Mark. "I'm going to ride him this time. Mr Cobbley said I could."

"I want to ride too," said Carol.

"No, you're too little. Mr Cobbley said so."

"He didn't."

"He did."

Carol stamped her foot. "He *didn't*!"

"Now stop it!" said Mum. "If you argue like that at Gran's, she'll pack you off home. Mark, you're the eldest. You must promise me you won't argue with your sister."

"I'll try not to," said Mark. "But it's Carol who starts it!"

"I do not!" said Carol.

"You *do*!"

"I do *not*!"

"STOP IT!" Dad spoke so loudly they both stopped at once. They stuffed their mouths with toast and marmalade and gave each other a kick under the table.

"Now let's go," said Dad. "It was a good idea waking us so early, Mark. If we start at once we shall be almost on the motorway before the rush hour."

The children hugged Mum and bundled into the back of the car, leaning out to wave and blow kisses. The streets were still quiet and the shops shut. In a very short time they had left the town behind and were out in the country. Fields were starred with daisies and the trees were bursting into leaf. She couldn't hear them above the noise of the car, but Carol knew that all the birds were singing as they built their nests. She looked out of the window and smiled. It was going to be a wonderful holiday.

Chapter two

It was a great journey. Mark and Carol did not argue once. They played the animal game, seeing who could score 100 first. You got one for a sheep, one for a cow, two for a horse, three for a pig, a cat or a dog, and four for a rabbit. Carol even saw a hedgehog, which counted for five.

Later, they felt thirsty. So they stopped at a motorway service station and had a can of Coke each and an ice cream. Then they raced back to the car. The day was getting hot by now and the traffic was heavy. Mark was sorry when they turned off the M5 because he loved racing the lorries. But Carol was glad. She loved the little narrow roads that wound up and down. She liked the glimpses from the hilltops of lambs in green fields. Then suddenly they both gave a shout for there was a notice ahead of them. It said they were in Devon.

"Not long now," said Dad. "We'll soon see the tidal river, and then the sea."

The first glimpse of the sea was always exciting. Today it was blue with little white waves breaking all over it. They turned

south. Soon the children began to remember the bridge across the river and the steep hill to the cliff top. They remembered the wide coast road that climbed and dipped. Then came the cottages and the village shop, where they turned left into Gran's lane. Two minutes more, and they saw Gran herself standing at the door of her cottage. In 30 seconds they were out of the car and Carol had run right into Gran's arms.

"Can I sleep in the little room where the roof comes down to the floor?" Carol said.

"Hi Gran," said Mark, pushing Carol aside and giving Gran a kiss. "Can we go to the sea this afternoon? Can I swim?"

Gran looked horrified. "In April?" she exclaimed. "I should have thought it was far too cold. What does your dad say?"

"They're tough," said Dad. "Cold water won't hurt them. How are you, Mum? It's good to be here again."

They carried in their cases and took them upstairs. Carol had the attic room where the roof came down to the floor. Mark had the room overlooking the sea where he could watch the ships steaming up and down the Bristol Channel. But they had not got long to unpack because lunch was ready. They clattered downstairs to the little kitchen, where Gran was serving up pizza and salad, followed by trifle.

Dad left soon after lunch. Then Gran got out her car, for the cliff road was long and steep. Mark and Carol flung the goggles, the snorkel, the spade, the bucket and some towels on to the back seat.

"Do we have to go in the car?" asked Mark. "Can't we run?"

"If you keep to the side of the road, you can," said Gran. "But *I'm* not running! The cliff road is long and steep. You'll be glad of the car coming back! Now, off you go!"

They raced down through the dark woods where the stream ran along beside them below the road. Then they came out into the sunshine where the cottages began and great drifts of primroses grew on the banks. Gran had driven behind them and parked the car where the road

became just a rocky path that led to the beach. The sun was shining and small waves were breaking in foam on the sand.

"Quick!" shouted Mark, flinging off his clothes. "Where's my snorkel?" He raced for the sea, but Carol was not in such a hurry. The water was very cold and she did not stay in it long. Instead, she and Gran built a huge sandcastle.

"How far does the water come?" asked Carol.

"Right up to the wall," said Gran, "and it's coming very fast. Look, there's hardly any sand left. We'll soon have to move the towels. Our castle isn't going to last long!"

Mark came up from the sea to help. They shovelled more sand on the back of the castle and put stones in front, but it was no good. It soon crumbled and the sea seemed to be running up the shore. The other people on the beach were packing up and leaving. The children were suddenly glad that they had not got to walk up that steep hill.

It had been a long, exciting day. By the time they reached home and had some tea, watched a bit of TV and visited the horse, they were quite tired. By seven o'clock, Carol's eyes were closing.

"You can't go to bed yet," said Mark. "It's much too early."

"It's the sea air," said Gran, "and getting up at the crack of dawn! Carol, why don't you go to bed? I'll come and tell you a story."

"Oh, yes," said Carol. She loved Gran's stories. Mark thought he was too old for stories at bedtime, but he did not mind listening to Carol's. He gave a great yawn.

"Think I'll go to bed too," he said. "And I might come in and listen to Carol's story. Is it about smugglers and wreckers?"

Gran laughed. "No," she said. "I'll tell you about them when we go to the wreck museum. Now, would you like a snack before bed?"

Half an hour later, Carol had snuggled down in bed. Gran was sitting beside her. Through the open attic window they could see the sky, still bright from the sunset. There was a wind blowing up from the sea. Carol wondered what it would be like on the beach with the dark waves breaking against the cliff. She gave a little shiver.

"Is it high tide now?" she asked.

"It will just have turned," said Gran. "There'll be plenty of sand tomorrow morning. Shall I tell you a story about a boat and a storm?"

There was a big bounce on the end of the bed. Mark had arrived, dressed in his pyjamas. "Tell me, too," he said, curling up under the blanket. So Gran told them about a dark night, long ago, when the wind came sweeping down from the hills, whipping up the waves. Twelve friends of

Jesus were caught in a storm as they tried to row across the lake. Gran said she thought they would have been very afraid their boat was going to sink. She said they must have wished *so* much that Jesus was with them. But Jesus had stayed behind.

Then suddenly one of them looked up and saw someone coming towards them, walking on the water! At first they were

very scared and thought it was a ghost. Then they saw that it was Jesus!

Mark interrupted the story then.

"I've heard this story before," he said. "And I don't believe it. No one could walk on the water."

"Well, *we* couldn't," said Gran. "But if Jesus was really God, then he made the sea and the land. And if you make something, you can do what you like with it."

"Yes. Do shut up, Mark," said Carol. "Go on, Gran. What happened?"

So Gran went on. "Peter, one of Jesus' friends, saw Jesus and he thought, I'd rather be with Jesus on the sea than without him in the boat! So he called out, 'If it's really you, tell me to come to you on the water.'

"'Come on!' said Jesus. Peter slipped over the side and he too walked on the water, looking hard at Jesus all the time. But suddenly he looked away and saw the great, black waves. He was very scared and began to sink. 'Save me, Lord!' he shouted.

"Jesus grabbed hold of his hand just in time. 'Why were you afraid?' he said. 'Why didn't you believe in me?'

"They walked back to the boat together. As soon as they got in, the wind stopped. Everything was safe and all right when Jesus was there. And it's still like that today," said Gran. "If Jesus is with us, loving us and looking after us, then everything is safe and happy. But we have to ask him."

The sky was quite dark now, and two stars were shining in at the window. Carol was nearly asleep. It had been a scary story and she was glad it had ended like it did, with everything all right. Everyone in the story was OK. They were loved, safe and happy because Jesus was there. She thought of the wind and the waves and the high tide. She wanted always to feel safe and happy too.

She would ask Gran to tell her more about Jesus another night.

Chapter three

The next three days passed happily. The children stayed on the beach when the sun shone. If it was dull or rainy they went to the farm and fed a motherless lamb with a bottle. A little late lamb was born one morning and they watched it take its first wobbly steps. Every evening they phoned home to ask if the baby had arrived. But it seemed to be taking its time. Still, they got news of the rabbits and told Mum and Dad what they were doing.

Every night when Carol was tucked in bed, Gran came and told her a story from the Bible. Carol was beginning to think that the Bible was a very interesting book with so many stories about Jesus. He seemed such a kind person, always helping people and making them well and happy. Gran said that although people could not see him, he was still here in the world, ready to help anyone who asked him. Mark still said he did not believe it but Gran said it was true. Still, Mark would rather have stories about wreckers and smugglers. But he always came and listened, curled up at the bottom of the bed. And, sometimes, when Gran stopped, he told her to go on.

The time raced by, and it was not till the fourth day that Mark and Carol had their first real argument. They were just finishing breakfast. Gran was talking to the milkman and they were alone.

"I'm going to see the horse," said Mark. "Tell Gran."

"No!" said Carol, standing in front of the door. "It's your turn to dry the dishes. Gran said we were to help in turns."

"I did it yesterday," said Mark. "Get out of the way."

"You did not!" shouted Carol. "I did *all* the tea things."

"Tea doesn't count. It's only a little bit. I did it at lunchtime so it's *your* turn."

"It's not!" yelled Carol.

"It is!"

"I'm not doing it!"

"Well, I'm not either! Get out of the way!"

"I'll tell Gran!"

"I don't care. Get out of the way or I'll—"

"Don't you *dare* push me!"

But he did. When Gran came back, they were fighting, punching and scratching.

Carol was smaller than Mark, but she could hit very hard when she was cross.

Gran pulled them apart. Carol started crying. Mark looked sulky.

"He hit me on the head!" sobbed Carol.

"And she hit me on the arm!" said Mark, showing Gran the red marks. "She's a cry baby... and it's *her* turn to dry the dishes!"

"I'm not and it isn't!"

"You are and it is!"

and the lambs were skipping round their mothers. Mark ran to catch up with Carol and Carol soon stopped sniffing. By the time they reached the shop they were happy again and planning how to spend their pocket money.

There was only one shop in the village and they had to wait some time to pay at the checkout. Mark stood in the queue with the basket, but Carol wandered outside and looked round. There was a path behind the shop leading up to some cottages. At the top of the hill was a caravan site. They had never been up there and Carol thought there would be an amazing view of the coast. Mark was sure to be ages; she would run a little way and see.

But she never got to the top of the hill because when she reached the gate of the more trouble. "But, of course, we could always go in and look at them…"

"Yes!" said Carol, pushing open the gate and dancing up the path. She knocked loudly at the door and a woman opened it.

"We've come to see the kittens," said Carol. "We've got a good home. We're staying with Mrs White; she's our gran."

"Well, the kittens are ready to go," said the woman. "Your gran's a friend of mine. She'd know how to look after a kitten. They're all out here in the woodshed."

Mark and Carol knelt down in the woodshed and forgot about everything else. There were four kittens. They had long, soft fur and round blue eyes. They were crawling in and out of their basket or scampering back to their mother for a feed. Carol picked up a grey kitten; Mark picked up a black one with four white paws and a white nose.

"We'll have this one," he said, "and I shall call him Tippet because of the white tips on his paws and nose."

"No," said Carol, "we're having this one, and I shall call him Fluff because he's so soft."

"No, we're not having that one!" said Mark. "I'm the eldest so I'm going to choose. I've made up my mind. I'll share Tippet with you."

But Carol wanted the grey kitten more than anything else in the world.

"I wish I'd come in to see them without you!" she cried. "I want *this* one."

The woman took away the kittens in a hurry. She was afraid the children might have a fight and pull them in half.

"Dear me!" she said. "I'm not giving you a kitten if you're going to argue over it like that. You can go back to your gran and ask her what she thinks. When you've made up your minds, tell her to come with you."

She led the children out into the garden. Then she went into the cottage and shut the door. Mark gave Carol a kick.

"You see, you've lost them both now!" he said angrily. "That woman will tell Gran we argued. Then Gran will say we can't have them. You always spoil everything, Carol."

"No I don't!" sobbed Carol, kicking back as hard as she could. "They were *my* kittens. I found them. I hate you! I'm going to run away. And I'll come back and get Fluff all by myself."

She was off, slamming the gate behind her. She began to run down the hill. Mark couldn't see which way she went because the trees hid her from view.

Chapter four

Mark waited for a few minutes, just to show Carol that he didn't care if she did run away. Then he walked back to the shop and looked round. He couldn't see her anywhere.

She was probably hiding, but he wished he knew where. She might have run very fast and turned the bend in the road that led to Gran's cottage. She might now be telling tales to Gran and Gran would think it was all his fault! And of course it wasn't, not at all. He was the eldest, and the black and white kitten was by far the prettiest. And he did *so* want to go and see the lighthouse. He sniffed and felt very sorry for himself.

On the other hand, Carol might have run into the field opposite the shop and be hiding behind the barn. He was quite sure that she would not have run down the twisty little road that led to the sea because she was afraid of the dark woods. When they were not arguing, he always held her hand when they ran between the trees. He didn't like them much himself.

He decided to search behind the barn. If she wasn't there, he would go home and peep round the kitchen door to see if she had arrived first. If she was not there, he would pretend they were playing outside and wait till she turned up. Carol was such a baby!

"Wait till I get her alone," he muttered. "I'll teach her! But not till after we've been to the lighthouse…"

But Carol wasn't behind the barn, or anywhere in the field. He walked a little way along, peering into the hedge. He did not find her, but he found a hedge sparrow's nest, beautifully woven from moss with five bright blue eggs in it. It was so beautiful that he almost forgot Carol. He waited quite a long time, crouching in the grass, until the sparrow came back. Then he tiptoed away, feeling rather sorry. If only they had not argued, he could have shown Carol that nest. She would have loved it.

He thought he had better go home with the basket and see what was happening. Gran would be wondering where he was. If he was nice to Carol, they might still go to Hartland Point. He hurried up the road and stuck his nose cautiously round the back door.

It was very quiet in the kitchen. Gran was all alone, doing the ironing. She

looked up and smiled. "At last!" she said. "I thought you'd got lost, and you had all my shopping with you! Where's Carol?"

"Er… she's playing outside. Can we go over to the farm for a bit?"

"Yes, for half an hour. We'll have lunch early and then set off to the lighthouse."

Mark ran to the farm but Carol wasn't there. He was beginning to get very worried indeed. Whatever would Gran say if she hadn't come back by lunchtime? And, anyway, where *was* she? For the first time he started to feel really bothered, not just about Gran and the lighthouse, but about Carol herself.

He went back to the shop but the girl on the checkout hadn't seen her. He stood at the top of the steep, winding road that led down to the sea and felt even more bothered. She couldn't have run down there all by herself. He was sure she couldn't. But half an hour was up and there was nothing to be done but to go back and tell Gran. He shuffled into the kitchen.

"Come along," said Gran. "Lunch is all ready and I've made some nice scones for tea. Where's Carol?"

Mark hung his head. "I can't find her," he muttered. "She ran away. I've looked everywhere for her."

"She ran away? But you said you were going to the farm. Did she run from the farm?"

"It was before that. She ran away from the shop. I've looked everywhere, honest I have."

"But you said she was playing outside. Just when did you lose her? Tell me at once, Mark. How long has she been gone?"

Mark knew from her voice that Gran was scared and he suddenly felt very scared too. He had to fight back the tears.

"I don't know," he said. "She just ran. I couldn't see where she went. We were on the hill behind the shop. She ran behind the trees. When I came down she wasn't there."

"Well, if she hasn't come home and she isn't at the farm, she must have run down to the sea. It was very naughty of you, Mark, not to tell me sooner. We must look for her right away. If we can't find her, we must phone the police."

Gran hurried to the garage and got the car. She called to the neighbour to be on the lookout in case Carol came back while they were away. Mark jumped into the car and they drove slowly down the road, looking to left and right. Neither of them said anything at all. Carol was nowhere in sight.

They reached the shop that sold groceries, ice creams, cups of tea and blue china mugs. They drove through the dark woods and past the primroses to the cottages. From there, the rocky footpath led down to the beach.

But there wasn't any beach. The tide had come in and the waves, blue and sparkling, were breaking against the cliff. Gran turned the car round and then went back to the shop. She stopped the car and spoke to a man and a woman who were drinking tea at a table outside the shop.

"We've lost a little girl of 8," said Gran. "Did you happen to notice a child by herself?"

The couple looked at each other.

"Yes," said the woman, "about an hour ago when we came up from the beach. Don't you remember, darling? A little girl ran past us; pretty little girl she was, with fair, curly hair. I thought her parents were down by the sea. But she can't be there now. The tide's in."

"You haven't seen her since?"

"No. But we were in the shop for a bit so maybe we didn't notice."

"Thank you." Gran's voice sounded strange and tight. Mark glanced up at her and noticed that her face had gone very pale. She seemed to have forgotten all about him.

"I suppose she could have run along into the next cove," said Gran. "The cliff is further back there and it may not be too late. We must ring the coastguard at once."

She went back into the shop. Mark stood in the road that turned into a rocky path, staring out over the sea. Where, oh where was Carol?

Chapter five

Where *was* Carol?

When she ran away from the garden where the kittens lived, she was so angry that she didn't really know what she was doing. She wanted to run and run and give Mark a big fright. If she didn't come back for a long time, Gran would be very cross with Mark for not looking after her. So she would run for a long way and get really properly lost.

She would run right down to the sea and hide behind the rocks. Mark would be carrying that heavy basket. He would never catch up with her. She was so angry that she hardly noticed the dark woods. She was much too busy thinking about that grey kitten – and hating Mark.

"Fluff, Fluff," she cried to herself, "I wanted you so badly. If only I'd never shown Mark! If only I'd just gone in alone and got you. I shan't go back, not for a long time. I *hate* him."

She ran right through the dark woods and came out into the sunshine. The clumps of primroses on the banks were like great yellow pools. She stopped to smell them and noticed some white violets sheltering under a fern. She smelt them too, but she did not pick them, because she thought they might wilt.

She had reached the cottages and looked down the path that led to the sea. She almost decided to go home. But she still had plenty of time before lunch. She would hide for a little while in case Mark came to look for her.

She would not go down to the beach because the tide was quite high and all the people were coming up. But there was a little path that ran along the bottom of the cliff for quite a long way. It seemed to turn a corner further on and Mark would never think of looking for her there.

It was fun running along that path on that bright April morning. There were seagulls nesting on the cliff. As she watched the swoop of their white wings, she almost forgot her troubles. She felt rather sorry. If only they hadn't argued,

she could have shown Mark the gulls'
nests. He would have loved that.

The path had turned a corner and she
suddenly found herself in another little
cove where the cliffs were much further
back. Here there was plenty of room and
lots of sand and the water seemed quite
far away. She had never been here before
and she felt quite excited. She would bring

Mark here as soon as they had become friends again. She thought it was even nicer than their own beach. She began to look for shells. There were little pools in the rocks too. They had pretty sea plants growing in them, and tiny crabs scuttling to and fro. It was so warm and quiet and sheltered that she felt almost sleepy. She had no idea how late it was getting.

It was only when she happened to look up that she noticed how much nearer the water had come. She felt a little bit scared. It must be nearly lunchtime, she thought, and she still had to climb that steep hill home. She suddenly wanted to get back as quickly as possible. Mark had had plenty of time to have a big, big fright. Gran had had plenty of time to have been very cross with him. She began to wonder whether Gran might be cross with her too.

She ran to the place where the path had turned the corner and then she forgot all about Mark and Gran and everything else. She just stood staring and staring. For ahead of her was nothing but water. The path was covered all the way to the bottom of the cliff and their beach wasn't there any more. The tide had come in and there was nothing at all but sparkling blue

water and little white waves breaking
against the rocks.

Carol felt very scared. She began to cry.
She wondered if the sea would come right
up to the cliffs in the new cove. If it did,
she would be drowned. She couldn't get
out either side. She tried to find a path up
the cliff, but the rocks were too steep for a
little girl to climb. She sat down on a big
rock and she had never felt so lonely and
afraid before.

She knew that if she waited long enough, the tide would turn and the path would be there again. But she did not know how far the water would reach in the cove where she was sitting. It was getting nearer and nearer, quite close to her sandals. She thought of her mother and father, the new baby and the rabbits. But they were far away and they couldn't help her. She thought of Gran and Mark. They would be out looking for her now, but how would they know where to look? She wanted Mark to come so badly! Mark would know what to do. She always felt safe when Mark was there. But how could he come when the path was covered with water?

Gran and Mark! She began to think about the cottage: the warm kitchen, the apple blossom in the garden. She thought about that cosy time, just before she went to sleep, when Gran sat beside her bed telling stories and Mark curled up under the blanket in his pyjamas. She remembered the first story Gran had told. She began to think about it. It was about the sea, not on a blue sparkly day like this, but on a dark night. There were 12 men who were very scared, just like she was. But Jesus had come, walking on the water. Then they

hadn't been scared any more. Everything was all right when Jesus came.

She remembered something else too. Gran had said that Jesus was still here, although people couldn't see him. She'd said that Jesus was ready to help anyone who asked him. Mark had said he didn't believe it, but Gran had said it was true. Gran knew more than Mark. Suppose Carol told Jesus that she needed to be rescued? Suppose he came to her, walking on the water? She didn't think he would, but she could at least try.

"Jesus," she said, closing her eyes because that was what Gran did when she prayed, "please come and help me. Don't let the water come right to where I am. Please help me to get out."

She opened her eyes but she was still alone. She began to think about Jesus.

Gran had said that he was very good. Carol knew that *she* wasn't good at all. She had argued with her brother. She had even had a fight with him! She shut her eyes again.

"Jesus, please help me," she said. "I know I'm not always very good. I've been horrible to Mark. I'm sorry. I'll let Mark have the black and white kitten."

She opened her eyes again and blinked. A boat was coming round the curve of the cliff. It was coming straight into the cove and she could hear the chug-chug of its engine. For a moment she thought it must be Jesus. But then she remembered that Jesus didn't come in a boat. He walked on the water! Well, *someone* was coming, anyway. She jumped up and shouted and waved with all her might.

The boat came right up close to her. The coastguard jumped out and lifted her into the boat.

"Now, what's this all about?" he said. "You nearly scared the life out of your gran and your brother! Don't you ever run off by yourself like that again!"

And Carol, holding tight to the side of the boat as it skimmed out of the cove, made up her mind that she never, never would.

Chapter six

Gran and Mark sat on a big rock, just above the waterline, waiting for the coastguard to come back. He had arrived very quickly after Gran had phoned him. He had agreed that it was possible that Carol had strayed into the next cove before the tide was right up. But, he had said, that cove would soon be covered and he'd better get going. He had started the engine and shot off round the corner.

Gran did not speak at all. She seemed to have forgotten about Mark, sitting so quietly beside her. He felt terribly lonely. He believed that if anything bad had happened to Carol, it was all his fault. Perhaps Gran was very angry with him and that was why she did not speak to him. He looked up at her and saw that her eyes were shut like when she prayed at night. He knew that she was praying for Carol.

I wonder if it does any good, thought Mark. He shut his eyes and began saying quietly to himself, "Please, God, if you're there, find Carol."

He started thinking about Carol. What if she never came back? It would be horrible without Carol. Whatever would Mum and Dad say? He suddenly felt very sorry that he had kicked her and been selfish. "If Carol comes back," he said to himself, "I'll be really nice to her. I'll even let her have the grey kitten."

Then he looked up. He saw the boat swing round the curve in the coastline, much sooner than they had expected.

Mark gave Gran such a push that she nearly fell sideways off the rock.

"Gran!" he yelled, jumping up. "It's coming. Look! Can you see her?"

They stood together shading their eyes against the sun. Suddenly Gran gave a great sigh and sat down.

"She's there," she said. "Thank God!"

Mark rushed to the entrance of the little bay where the waves lapped against the wall. The coastguard drew in. He waved cheerily to Gran and lifted Carol on to the steps. She and Mark stood with the water right over their sandals and hugged each other. Then Carol ran to Gran.

"Gran," she said in a surprised voice, "why are you crying? Can't you see I'm safe?"

"Yes, I can," said Gran, holding her tight. "That's why I'm crying." And then they all started laughing instead.

They were all quiet driving back up the hill. Mark and Carol knew that they had both been very naughty. If Gran was going to be cross they really could not blame her. But Gran was not cross. She just seemed very tired.

We've all had such a fright, thought Gran. Let's all be happy now. Perhaps we will talk about it another time, or perhaps they have learned their lesson without any talking.

It was too late to go to Hartland Point, so they decided to go the next day. But they all enjoyed their lunch. When they had finished, Carol was so tired that she fell asleep in the armchair. Then they went to the farm and fed the calves and they both had a ride on the horse. Mark did not

say that Carol was too little. He helped her on and off and held the reins so that the horse would not trot too fast.

They went to bed tired but happy. When Gran came for the goodnight story, both Mark and Carol felt that it would be a special sort of story. So they both listened hard. It was about ten men and they all had a terrible illness called leprosy.

"In some places in the world, people still get this disease," said Gran, "but now it can be cured. There was no medicine for it then. They became covered with spots and sores. Then they had to leave their homes and towns in case anyone else caught it. They had to live out on the hills and no one would go near them. Their families would leave food for them to pick up. But these ten men heard about Jesus. They came and stood waiting for him on the hillside. They didn't dare come too near the road. When they saw Jesus coming they all started shouting at the tops of their voices, 'Jesus, Master, have pity on us!'

"Jesus stopped. He was not afraid of leprosy. He just wanted to help the men. He told them to go back to their homes. He knew that, by the time they got there, they would all be well.

"And they believed him. They all started rushing down the road. As they ran, their illness was healed. Their spots and sores disappeared. They were going home strong and well.

"All except one! He suddenly stopped. He was a stranger from another country. Then he turned round and came running back to Jesus! He fell down in front of him and began to thank him with all his heart.

"Jesus was rather sad. 'I healed ten,' he said. 'Where are the other nine? Has only one stopped to say thank you?'

"But he was glad about the one. 'You may get up and go,' said Jesus. 'Your faith has made you well.'

"And the tenth man went home much happier than the others. The others had been healed, but the tenth had talked to Jesus and come to know him. And he had made Jesus glad by saying thank you."

"Shall we say thank you because I was rescued?" asked Carol. "You know, Gran, when I was there in that cove, I remembered about Jesus walking on the water. I asked him to help me, and then I saw the boat."

"It wasn't Jesus, it was the coastguard," said Mark.

"But that's how God answers our prayers," said Gran. "We can't see Jesus walking about on earth any more. But his love and power are still here, working through other people. It was God who made those people outside the shop notice where you had gone, Carol. It was God who made the coastguard come so quickly. It was God who helped you to wait quietly instead of trying to climb the cliff or swim or do anything silly. We were praying and he was helping us all the time. So we must certainly thank him."

They all shut their eyes. Gran thanked God for looking after Carol and keeping her safe. Carol remembered that terrible moment when she knew that the water was all round her. Gran and Mark remembered how they had sat on that rock and wondered if Carol had drowned. But it had all come right in the end. Even Mark knew that someone bigger than them had been there, listening to them and helping them.

And Mark and Carol both remembered something else. Since coming home from the beach, no one had talked about the kittens at all. Those kittens needed a lot of thinking about!

Chapter seven

Next morning Mark awoke to the sun pouring in through his bedroom window. It was a perfect day for Hartland Point and he jumped out of bed.

"Gran!" he shouted. "Let's have breakfast soon and let's take a picnic to the lighthouse."

Gran was in the kitchen in her dressing gown, making herself a cup of tea. She promised they would set off as early as possible.

"I could go to the shop by myself this morning," said Mark, "and Carol could help you get ready. It would be quicker that way. Can we have crisps with our picnic, Gran? Mum won't let us eat crisps at home... well, only sometimes."

"All right," said Gran, "and, as a great treat, we might finish up with a cream tea at a farm. But Carol likes going to the shop too, so we must wait and see what she wants."

To Gran's surprise, Carol seemed quite pleased with the idea of Mark going shopping alone. In fact, she seemed in rather a hurry to get him out of the house. As soon as he had left, she pulled Gran down on the sofa beside her.

"Gran," she said. "It's about the kittens."

"What kittens?" asked Gran.

"The kittens we had a fight about," said Carol. "We didn't tell you, but that's why I ran away. They're in the house up the hill behind the shop. They're free. You don't have to pay anything. I wanted the grey one – he's so sweet, Gran, the sweetest little kitten you ever saw. But Mark

wanted the black and white one. So we had a big argument and I ran away, and then..."

Carol was suddenly quiet.

"Well?" said Gran. "Go on."

"Well, when I was on the beach," said Carol very slowly, "I just thought I didn't want to argue with Mark any more, and I thought I'd let him have the black and white kitten after all. And Gran, could we go and get it *now*? Could we go across the field so we shan't meet him? You see, I want it to be a surprise."

"But," said Gran, "what will your mum say? Does she want a kitten as well as a new baby?"

"She won't mind," said Carol. "There's lots of room for both at home. And if she really says we can't have it, you could keep it, Gran! We'd play with it when we come to stay."

"Well," said Gran, "I wouldn't mind. I thought I heard a mouse in the shed the other day. I did think about getting a cat. Let's go at once, before Mark gets back."

They found a basket with a lid. Then they went out through the back gate and crossed the field. It was a longer way but much prettier. The dew still lay on the grass, silver and shining. The daisies and dandelions were beginning to open their faces to the sunshine. Carol walked slowly and she did not say anything at all. It was going to be very hard to see that grey kitten again and then leave it behind. As they came near to the cottage she took Gran's hand and held it tight.

The woman who had showed them the kittens the day before had gone out. Her husband opened the door. He was pleased to see Gran.

"Come for a kitten, have you?" he said. "My wife told me about your two young'uns yesterday. Made up your mind now, have you? Well, looks like we've found homes for *two* kittens today. A lad came in not long ago and took one, just after my wife went out."

Carol gasped. Supposing someone had taken the black and white one and she couldn't give Mark a surprise after all? She ran into the woodshed. It was all right! The black and white one was still there, clawing over the side of the basket. It was the grey kitten which had gone and Carol was glad. It would have been hard to see Fluff and then to leave him behind.

She held Tippet in her arms. He was very soft and fluffy. He looked up at her with big, baby-blue eyes. She stroked him softly. "Sweet little Tippet," she whispered. "You are not quite as nice as Fluff but I love you very much." Then she grabbed Gran's hand. "Gran, come quick," she cried. "I want to show Mark. He'll be home by now."

They hurried home up the road, carrying the kitten hidden in the basket. When they reached the cottage, Mark was hanging over the gate, looking very pleased with himself.

"Where have you been?" he said. "I've been looking everywhere for you. Carol, you'd better come into the kitchen 'cos I've got a surprise for you."

"I've got a surprise for you, too!" said Carol. She rushed into the kitchen and there, in the middle of the table, was the grey kitten, lapping milk out of a saucer.

"It's Fluff!" cried Carol. "And here's Tippet!" She opened the basket and Tippet

leapt out and tried to push Fluff away from the milk. They both jumped into the saucer and the milk went all over the tablecloth. The kittens stuck their tails in the air and lapped the milk up.

"For goodness' sake, put them on the floor," said Gran who thought, for a moment, that she was seeing double. "Look what they've done to my tablecloth! They can't drink out of my best china tea service, either. Mark, there's a tin plate over on the sink. Until they are

house-trained, they must sleep in the shed. I don't know what your mum is going to say about it all."

"Can we take the kittens on the picnic?" said Mark.

"We *couldn't* leave them behind," said Carol.

So, when they had made some sandwiches and packed the picnic and swimming things, they set off. Mark, Carol, Tippet and Fluff all sat in the back of the car. The kittens travelled in a big cardboard box lined with an old woolly pullover. They snuggled down and looked very warm and comfortable.

They reached the lighthouse and had lunch. Then Mark and Carol and the kittens played among the daisies. In the afternoon, they went to a little beach. Mark and Carol both swam while Gran sat on a rock and the kittens rolled in the sand. Then they had a yummy cream tea at a farm. What a beautiful day it's been, thought Carol.

All day Mark felt love for Carol because she had given him Tippet. And Carol felt loving toward Mark because he had given her Fluff. Because they were loving, they were happy. And that, thought Carol, was why it was such a beautiful day.

Chapter eight

When they came home, they phoned Mum. Gran spoke first. Of course, Mark and Carol could only hear what was being said at one end of the phone. But they more or less knew what was happening by listening to Gran.

"How are things going, dear?" asked Gran. "Not long?… Good… Oh, they're fine, but they wanted me to ask you something. Would you mind if they each brought home a kitten?… Well, yes, I know and I'm sorry, but it was a mistake. They each got one for the other… Yes, it was meant to be only one; it was all a mistake. I'll write and explain… No, the kittens won't be having kittens of their own, they're both males… Yes, dear, I do realise there's going to be a baby in the house. Yes, I know it's all an extra expense but I'll help pay for the cat food... Well, just think it over, dear, and let us know."

Mark grabbed the phone and Carol listened anxiously.

"Mum, it will be all right about the baby," he said, very fast and loud. "I know cats like to sit where babies are. But I've got a friend whose mum had a baby and she kept the cat off it by putting up a little net... OK Mum, ask Dad, and tell us tomorrow, but please say yes!"

Carol snatched the phone from him. "Mum," she squealed, "they're the sweetest little kittens you ever saw! Their names are Fluff and Tippet. And Mum, there was only going to be one and we argued. I ran away and the tide came up and I was nearly drowned. The coastguard

rescued me. Then we both went and got the other one by mistake... No, Mum, it's all right, I didn't drown! I'm all right... I was just telling you..."

Gran took the phone from Carol.

"Carol's fine," she said firmly, "I'll write and tell you all about it. Just let us know at once if the baby comes. Bye now and God bless. We'll phone tomorrow."

But they didn't phone the next day because Dad phoned them first. And it wasn't about kittens. When they heard Gran's phone ring, Mark and Carol went on eating their tea because they didn't think it would be a call from home. Then they heard what Gran was saying.

"A little boy!" cried Gran. "Oh, I'm so very thankful... you're naming him after Grandpa? How lovely! How's the new mum?... Splendid!"

"It's a boy," whispered Mark. "Yes!"

"I don't mind," said Carol, and she really didn't.

They spoke to Dad on the phone and he told them both about Richard John, who was being named after Grandpa. Richard John weighed nine pounds three ounces and had lots of dark hair and a very loud voice.

When Dad had finished talking, Carol said, "And about the kittens? Can we have them?"

"Kittens?" said Dad. "What kittens?"

"Our kittens, Fluff and Tippet. Did Mum forget to tell you?"

"Well, she's been rather busy, hasn't she?"

"Well, can we have them, Dad? One kitten each?"

"Oh sure, if you'll look after them. A couple of kittens shouldn't be too much trouble. Have them ready in a box when I come on Friday."

"Friday!" cried Carol. "That's the day after tomorrow!" She turned to Gran. "Couldn't we go home tomorrow, Gran? I just can't *wait* to see the baby."

Mark looked thoughtful. He went to Gran and put his arms round her.

"It's not that we want to leave you, Gran," he said. "We've had a really good time. It's just that we're longing to see the baby. Couldn't you come with us?"

Gran rumpled his hair. "It's all right, Mark," she said. "I understand. I'm longing to see the baby too. I was hoping you might all come and stay in the summer holidays. That's less than three months away."

The children thought that this was a lovely plan and, after all, the time went quickly. They went into the town of Bideford the next morning and bought presents for the baby with their pocket money. They bought a bib with a robin on it and a rattle with a bell inside.

In the afternoon, they had a last swim. Then it was time to say goodbye to the farmer and the animals. They packed their things and watched the kittens have their supper. Then, at last, Carol was in bed and Mark was sitting cross-legged at the other end with the blanket round him. Gran leaned back in the armchair. She looked quite tired.

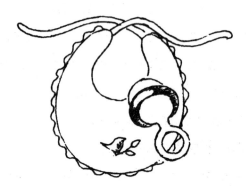

"Tomorrow," said Carol, wriggling her toes, "I shall be holding the baby."

"And me," said Mark. "You've got to take turns."

"What a happy baby he'll be!" said Gran quickly, before an argument could start. "And how blessed he is to be born into a family like yours, with a loving mother and father, brother and sister!"

"And two kittens," said Carol.

"And four rabbits," said Mark.

"And all our toys," said Carol. "Oh, I just can't wait! Gran, tell us a story, a special one because it's our last night."

"All right," said Gran. "We've been talking about the baby born into your family, so I'll tell you about a man who wanted to be born again."

"How silly," said Mark.

"You couldn't be born *again*," said Carol.

"Wait and see," said Gran.

She told them how the religious leaders of the country where Jesus lived became very jealous of Jesus. "Jesus was healing ill people and making the blind see. So of course everyone loved him and followed him and no one listened to the ordinary teachers. Everyone wanted Jesus.

"So the leaders and teachers got together and they made a plan. They told the people that Jesus was a wicked man and they must not go to him or listen to him. But one leader, called Nicodemus, wanted to listen. He knew that Jesus was good and loving but he was afraid to be seen visiting him. So he waited till it was quite dark and then he crept along the streets and knocked at the door.

"'Come in,' said Jesus.

'Sir,' said Nicodemus, 'I know that God has sent you, and I want to know how you do all these wonderful things.'

"Jesus said to him, 'If you want to understand, you must be born again.'"

Mark interrupted the story. "That's really silly! I said so before."

"Gran, what did Jesus mean?" said Carol.

"That's just what Nicodemus wanted to know," said Gran. "He was like Mark.

We've been talking about your baby, born into your family, belonging to Mum and Dad. Jesus is God's Son. When we come to know Jesus and love him, then we become God's children too. God becomes our heavenly Father. We are born into God's family and all the other people who love Jesus are like our brothers and sisters. We all love and help each other."

"So we've got to know Jesus before we can become God's children," said Carol thoughtfully.

"Yes. And shall I tell you how to know Jesus?" asked Gran.

"Yes, please," said Carol.

"We've just got to ask him," said Gran. "We can tell God we want to belong to him, and live his way. Then we can call God our heavenly Father and he makes us part of his family."

They talked for a little longer and Gran prayed. She thanked God for the new baby. And she asked that Mark and Carol would understand what it meant to be born into God's family. Then she tucked Carol up and kissed them both goodnight. "Go to sleep quickly," she said, "and then it will be tomorrow."

Mark went to his room. He knelt at his window with his arms on the sill. He looked out at the black Channel and the great dark sky above it. There were stars shining, millions of miles away. It was all so big and wide that it made him feel a bit small and lonely. He thought perhaps it would be good to know that he belonged to a heavenly Father who guided the stars and the sea – but who still cared about one boy.

Carol snuggled down under the blankets and thought about the baby: Our family… God's family… Mum and Dad, Mark and me and Richard John… Fluff, Tippet and the rabbits and a loving heavenly Father… it's nice to belong…

Then Carol fell asleep.